JIMMIE JOHNSON

by Connie Colwell Miller

NASCAR HEROES

Published by ABDO Publishing Company, PO Box 398166, Minneapolis, MN 55439. Copyright © 2013 by Abdo Consulting Group, Inc. International copyrights reserved in all countries. No part of this book may be reproduced in any form without written permission from the publisher. SportsZone™ is a trademark and logo of ABDO Publishing Company.

Printed in the United States of America,
North Mankato, Minnesota
112012
012013

 THIS BOOK CONTAINS AT LEAST 10% RECYCLED MATERIALS.

Editor: Chrös McDougall
Series Designer: Becky Daum

Photo Credits: Tyler Barrick/Getty Images, cover, title; Autostock/Russell LaBounty/AP Images, cover; Will Lester/AP Images, 4-5, 30 (bottom, right); Terry Renna/AP Images, 6-7; Chuck Burton/AP Images, 8-9; Coeur d'Alene Press/Ben Brewer/AP Images, 10-11; Nick Wass/AP Images, 12-13; John Cordes/WireImage/Getty Images, 14-15, 16-17; Nell Redmond/AP Images, 15; Streeter Lecka/Getty Images, 18-19; AP Images, 18, 30 (top); Keith Shimada/AP Images, 20; Greg McWilliams/AP Images, 21; Mary Schwalm/AP Images, 22-23, 31; Isaac Brekken/AP Images, 24-25; Ed Zurga/AP Images, 26; Karen Wagner/AP Images, 27, 30 (bottom, left); Cal Sports Media/AP Images, 28-29

Cataloging-in-Publication Data
Colwell Miller, Connie.
 Jimmie Johnson / Connie Colwell Miller.
    p. cm. -- (NASCAR heroes)
Includes bibliographical references and index.
ISBN 978-1-61783-664-0
1. Johnson, Jimmie, Carl, 1975- --Juvenile literature. 2. Automobile racing drivers--United States--Biography--Juvenile literature. I. Title.
796.72092--dc21
 [B]
                                                                            2012946321

CONTENTS

A Record-Shattering Win 5

On Track to Win 10

Jimmie's Big Break 14

First-Time Champ 18

Breaking More Records 22

A Legend 26

Timeline 30
Glossary 31
Index 32

Jimmie Johnson dominated throughout the 2009 Sprint Cup season.

A RECORD-SHATTERING WIN

In 2009, Jimmie Johnson was outracing everyone in National Association for Stock Car Auto Racing (NASCAR). He had already won six races in the Sprint Cup Series. Only three races remained in the Chase. Then bad luck hit.

Johnson spun out in the third lap of the Dickies 500. His car smashed against the inside wall of the track. The car was badly damaged. It looked like Johnson might not be able to finish the race. His crew worked on the car for more than an hour. Then Johnson came back. But he finished last among those who completed the race. The competition for the Sprint Cup championship again appeared to be wide open.

Johnson's crew works on his car during a 2009 race.

FAST FACT

Since 2004, the Chase has determined NASCAR's Cup Series champion. Jimmie Johnson qualified for the Chase every year through 2012.

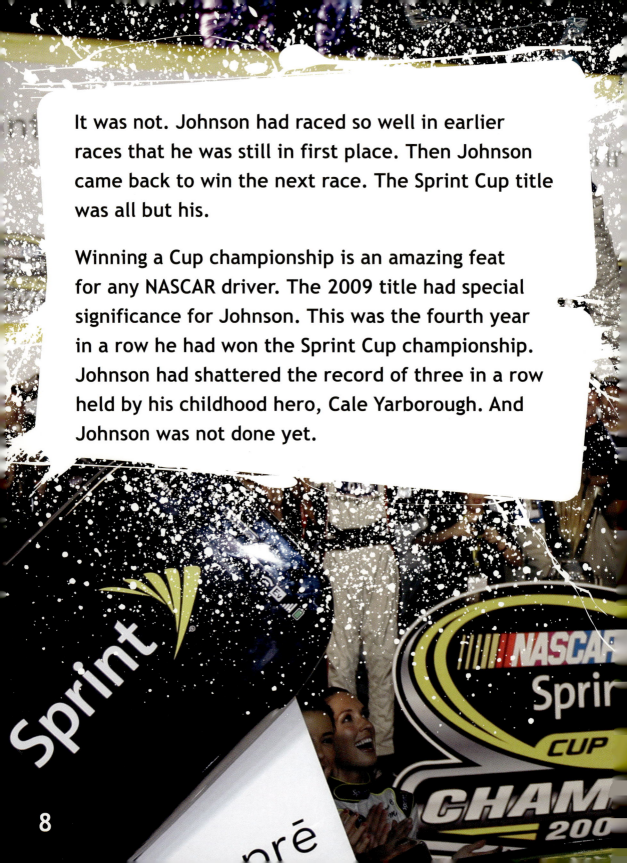

It was not. Johnson had raced so well in earlier races that he was still in first place. Then Johnson came back to win the next race. The Sprint Cup title was all but his.

Winning a Cup championship is an amazing feat for any NASCAR driver. The 2009 title had special significance for Johnson. This was the fourth year in a row he had won the Sprint Cup championship. Johnson had shattered the record of three in a row held by his childhood hero, Cale Yarborough. And Johnson was not done yet.

FAST FACT
Cale Yarborough won his third Cup Series championship in a row in 1978.

Johnson celebrates after winning the 2009 Sprint Cup championship.

ON TRACK TO WIN

Jimmie Johnson was born on September 17, 1975, in El Cajon, California. As a young boy, Jimmie loved surfing and dirt bike racing.

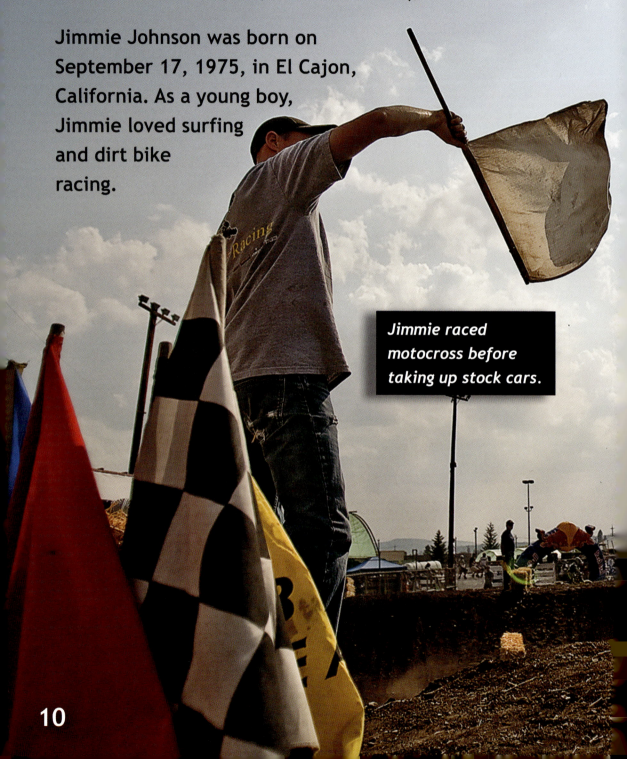

Jimmie raced motocross before taking up stock cars.

Jimmie started racing motorbikes when he was only five years old. In his youth, Jimmie won many motocross races. However, a broken knee at age 12 ended his motocross career.

FAST FACT

In 1992, 1993, and 1994, Jimmie Johnson won the national motocross championship.

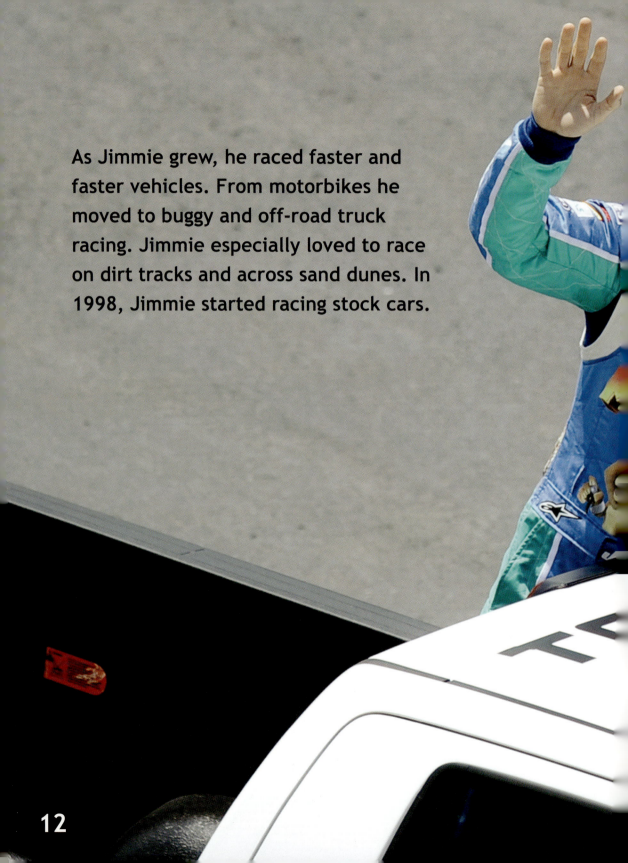

As Jimmie grew, he raced faster and faster vehicles. From motorbikes he moved to buggy and off-road truck racing. Jimmie especially loved to race on dirt tracks and across sand dunes. In 1998, Jimmie started racing stock cars.

Jimmie wears a rainbow wig during introductions for a 2012 race in Delaware.

FAST FACT
Early in his career, Jimmie Johnson was named Rookie of the Year in three different off-road racing series.

JIMMIE'S BIG BREAK

Johnson began racing in NASCAR's second-level series in 1998. NASCAR champion Jeff Gordon had been watching Johnson's car races. Gordon could tell Johnson was a natural behind the wheel. Gordon and NASCAR owner Rick Hendrick invited Johnson to drive for their new NASCAR team.

Johnson races in 2002.

FAST FACT
Jeff Gordon became Jimmie Johnson's teammate. He also became a part-owner of Johnson's car.

Johnson and Jeff Gordon in 2002

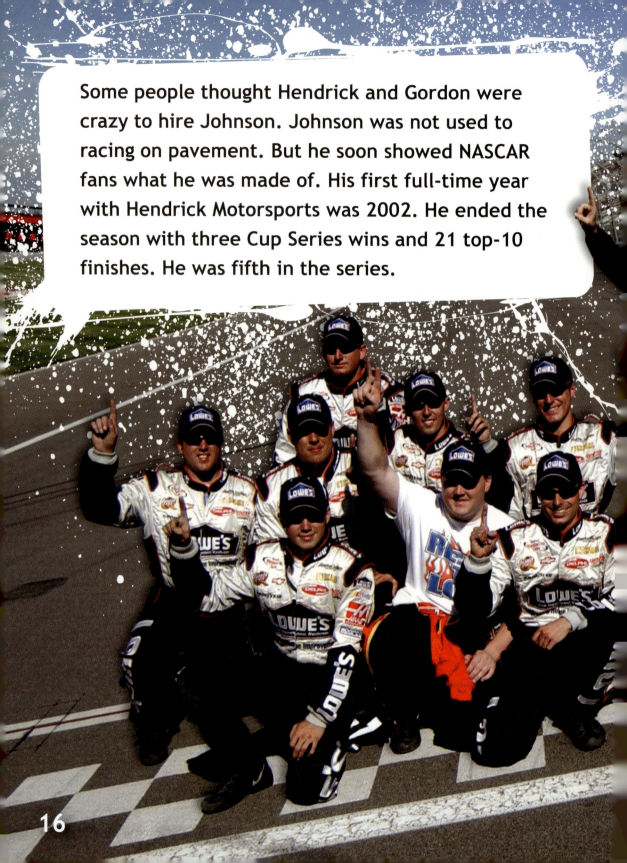

Some people thought Hendrick and Gordon were crazy to hire Johnson. Johnson was not used to racing on pavement. But he soon showed NASCAR fans what he was made of. His first full-time year with Hendrick Motorsports was 2002. He ended the season with three Cup Series wins and 21 top-10 finishes. He was fifth in the series.

FAST FACT

Jimmie Johnson won the pole at the Daytona 500 in 2002. It was just his fourth Cup Series start.

Johnson and his crew pose at the California Speedway after Johnson won a 2002 race there.

FIRST-TIME CHAMP

Johnson soon became a true NASCAR star. In both 2003 and 2004, he finished second in the Cup Series. But the number-one spot remained just out of reach.

Johnson and Chandra Janway

FAST FACT

Jimmie Johnson married Chandra Janway in 2004. They had a daughter named Genevieve in 2010.

Johnson cruises at a 2004 race at Darlington Raceway in South Carolina.

Johnson edges out Matt Kenseth for the win at a 2006 race in Las Vegas.

Johnson performs a burnout after winning a 2006 race at Talladega Superspeedway.

Johnson dropped to fifth in 2005. But 2006 proved to be his year to shine. As he grew used to the feel of the pavement, he got faster and more confident. That year, he grabbed five wins and 13 top-five finishes. He amazed fans and drivers alike by taking home his first Cup Series championship.

BREAKING MORE RECORDS

Johnson's next several years were like a dream come true for any NASCAR driver. He won the Cup Series championship in 2007, 2008, 2009, and 2010. No driver had ever won five championship titles in a row. Johnson was unstoppable.

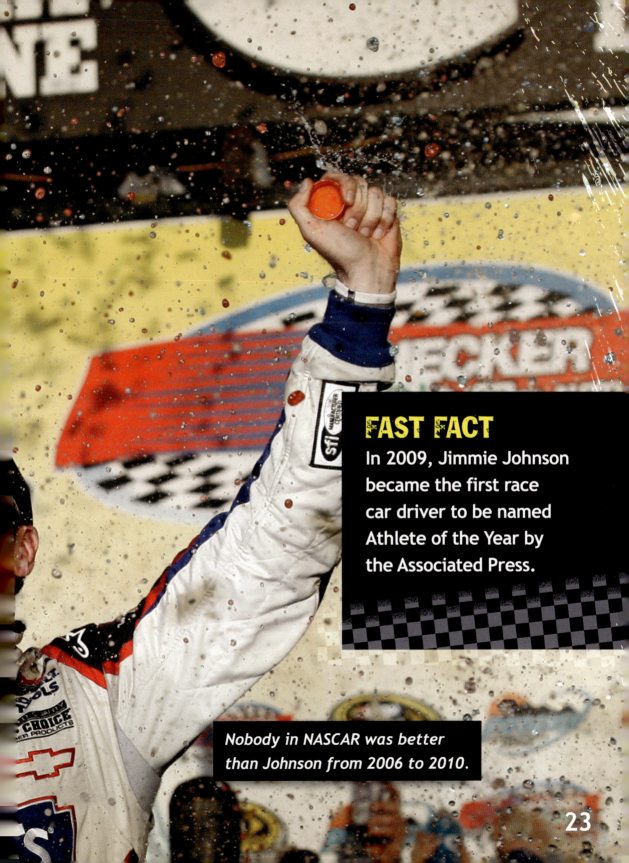

FAST FACT

In 2009, Jimmie Johnson became the first race car driver to be named Athlete of the Year by the Associated Press.

Nobody in NASCAR was better than Johnson from 2006 to 2010.

Johnson leads Greg Biffle during a 2010 race in Las Vegas.

In 2011, Johnson and his team came in sixth overall. That is a very high finish for most NASCAR drivers. For Johnson, it was his worst year in NASCAR. He was motivated to do better.

A LEGEND

Johnson's driving talent is legendary. Only two other NASCAR drivers in history have won five or more championships. Yet only Johnson won his five championship titles in a row!

Johnson leads a 2011 race at Kansas Speedway.

FAST FACT

Jimmie Johnson and Hendrick Motorsports became the third major US sports team to win five championships in a row. The Boston Celtics and the New York Yankees also achieved this feat.

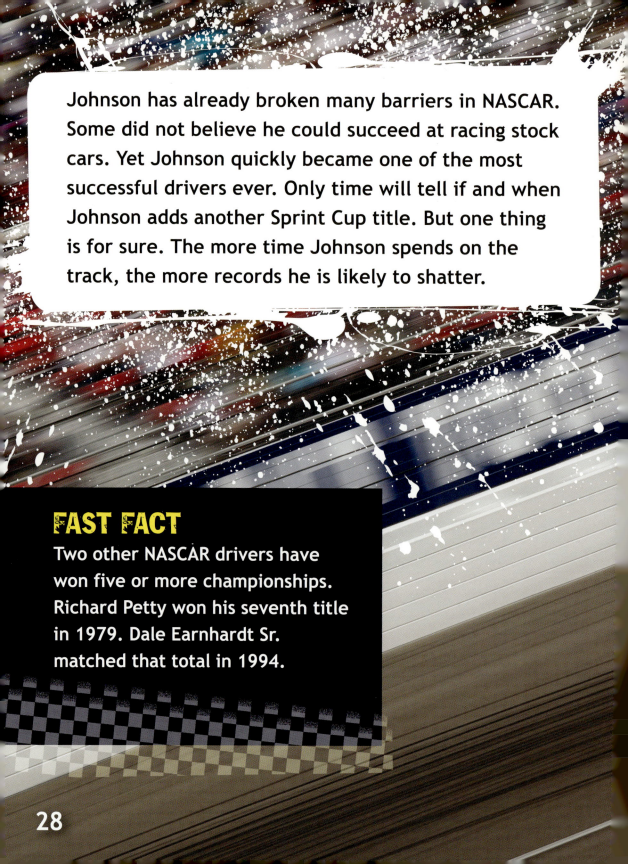

Johnson has already broken many barriers in NASCAR. Some did not believe he could succeed at racing stock cars. Yet Johnson quickly became one of the most successful drivers ever. Only time will tell if and when Johnson adds another Sprint Cup title. But one thing is for sure. The more time Johnson spends on the track, the more records he is likely to shatter.

FAST FACT

Two other NASCAR drivers have won five or more championships. Richard Petty won his seventh title in 1979. Dale Earnhardt Sr. matched that total in 1994.

The future is bright for Johnson.

TIMELINE

1975
Jimmie Johnson is born on September 17 in El Cajon, California.

2002
Johnson completes his first full-time season with Hendrick Motorsports.

2004
Johnson marries former model Chandra Janway.

2006
Johnson wins his first Cup Series title.

2007
Johnson wins his second Cup Series title.

2008
Johnson wins his third Cup Series title.

2009
Johnson wins his fourth Cup Series title. This win shatters the previous record of three in a row set by Cale Yarborough.

2010
Johnson wins his fifth Cup Series title in a row.

GLOSSARY

Chase
The last 10 races of the NASCAR Cup Series. Only the top 10 drivers and two wild cards qualify to race in the Chase.

Cup Series
NASCAR's top series for professional stock car drivers. It has been known as the Sprint Cup Series since 2008.

Daytona 500
The most famous stock car race in the world and one of the races in the Sprint Cup Series.

motocross
Motorcycle racing on unpaved roads or tracks.

off-road
Roads or tracks made of dirt, gravel, or other unpaved surfaces.

owner
The person who owns a racing team. This person hires everyone on the team, including the driver and the crew.

pole
The fastest time in qualifying.

series
A racing season that consists of several races.

start
Races in which the driver participates from the beginning.

stock car
Race cars that resemble models of cars that people drive every day.

INDEX

Associated Press Athlete of the Year, 23

Biffle, Greg, 24

California Speedway, 17
Chase, 5, 7
childhood, 10-11
crash, 6

Darlington Raceway, 19
daughter, 19
Daytona 500, 17
Dickies 500, 6

Earnhardt, Dale, Sr., 28

First Cup Series championship, 21
first stock car race, 12

Gordon, Jeff, 14-16

Hendrick Motorsports, 14-16, 27

Janway, Chandra, 18-19
joining first NASCAR team, 14

Kansas Speedway, 26
Kenseth, Matt, 20

Marriage, 19
motocross, 10-11

National Association for Stock Car Auto Racing (NACSAR), 5, 7-8, 14, 16, 18, 22-23, 25, 26, 28

Petty, Richard, 28

Records and firsts, 8, 22-23, 26, 27, 28
Rookie of the Year, 13

Sprint Cup Series, 4-9, 16-18, 21-22, 28

Talladega Superspeedway, 21

Yarborough, Cale, 8-9